Now I'm a Bird

Sue Ganz-Schmitt

illustrated by Renia Metallinou

ALBERT WHITMAN & COMPANY
Chicago, Illinois

To Tom (thanks for the "bird's-eye" view on writing),
Cheryl, who always lifts me up, and to my darling nestmates—
Jensen, India, and Martin.
—SS

To Nikolas and Christos.
The nicest kids I've ever met!
—RM

Library of Congress Cataloging-in-Publication data is on file with the publisher.

Text copyright © 2020 by Sue Ganz-Schmitt

Illustrations copyright © 2020 by Albert Whitman & Company

Illustrations by Renia Metallinou

First published in the United States of America in 2020 by Albert Whitman & Company

ISBN 978-0-8075-2329-2 (hardcover)

ISBN 978-0-8075-2328-5 (ebook)

Printed in China

10 9 8 7 6 5 4 3 2 1 WKT 24 23 22 21 20

Design by Carla Weise

For more information about Albert Whitman & Company,

visit our website at www.albertwhitman.com.

I didn't mean to be a bird.
It just happened.
Feather by feather.

I tried to hide them.

But Mom found out.

More useless feathers grew.
And more and more.

Soon everyone noticed.

"Why do I have to look
so fluffy?" I cried.

Dad said, "I love your plumage, honey."
Mom said, "Julianna, you are beautiful.
Just be yourself!"

I tried, but people stared
and stayed away.
Even my friends.

At ballet...

and birthday parties...

and at the beach.

By the end of summer,
the rest of my feathers filled in.
Like one big feather duster.

"I'm NOT going back to school," I said.
"Some kids are mean to birds."

Mom sent a letter
to the parents.

Dear parents,
My daughter Julianna
looks like a bird.
It's a rare and beautiful
condition.
Please discuss this
with your child.
Thank you.

"You've got this," said Dad on the first day of school. "I know you can wing it!"

The kids in my class had questions.

Two big kids from Room G chased me at recess. That's when I figured out feathers can be very helpful.

Principal Harrell called me to come down...

"VERY CAREFULLY, PLEASE!"

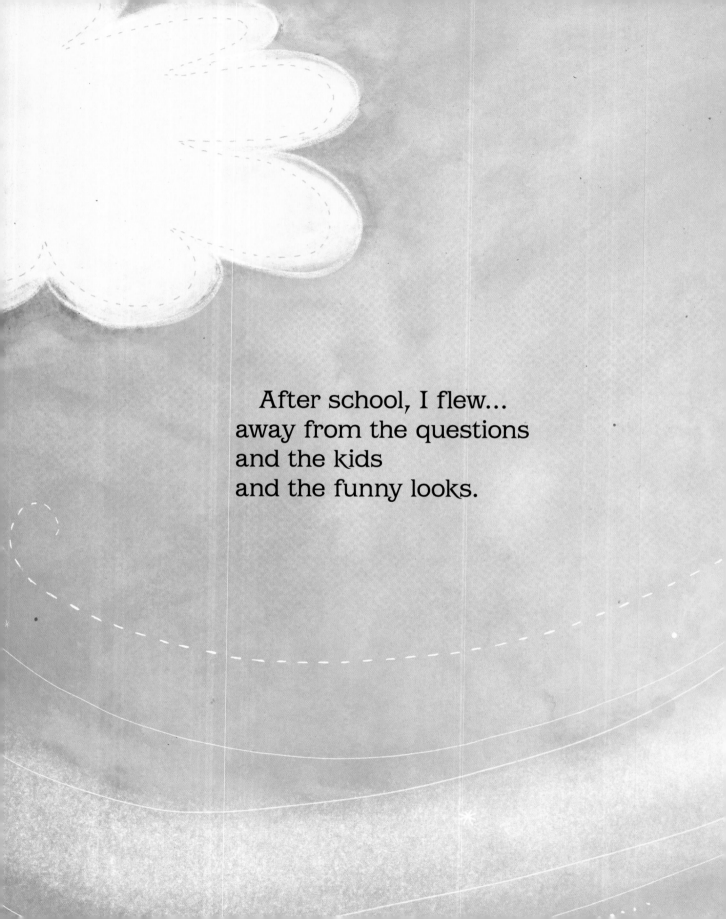

After school, I flew...
away from the questions
and the kids
and the funny looks.

Higher
and higher
and higher.

First it was like
being a prima ballerina
in the sky!

Whirling and twirling,
lighter than the wind.

But want to know
a secret?

Then it wasn't so grand.
I didn't have a flock.

And the cold gray clouds
gave me goose bumps.

I wanted my
warm nest.

The next day,
the Room G kids
wanted to fly me
around like a kite.

"NO!" I said.

They teased me until my feathers shook.

But when I looked down, I used my new bird's-eye view. Those big kids didn't look so big. And their words sounded very small.

I stretched my wings and swooped over them.

"Stop it!" I said.
"Birds are people too!"

"Yes, they are!" said a girl named Daphne.
"Thank you," I said.

Daphne stared hard at my feathers
and said, "I really like them."
"Me too," said a boy named Geo.
"They're very iridescent!"

"Thanks," I said. "I guess I like them too. Want to play?"
That's when I spotted Daphne's legs...

"I didn't mean to be a lizard," she said.
"It just happened."
   "We're all something." I said.

"That's for sure," said Geo.
"We're all something."

Now when the bell rings, we flock together...

In our fur

and scales
and feathers,

wild and wonderful.